HOW THE WORLD WAS SAVED
& OTHER NATIVE AMERICAN TALES

RETOLD AND ILLUSTRATED BY PIERS HARPER

A B C
London

To Kate and Brian

Text and illustrations copyright © 1994 Piers Harper
First published in 1994 by **ABC**, **All Books for Children**,
a division of The All Children's Company Ltd,
33 Museum Street, London WC1A 1LD

Printed and bound in Singapore

British Library Cataloguing in Publication Data
Harper, Piers
How the World Was Saved
I. Title
823

ISBN 1-85406-184-4

How the World Was Saved

Introduction

Long before scientists rationalized and ordered the universe, people needed to make sense of the oftentimes frightening and confusing world around them. Stories were told to explain such things as life, death, the cycles of nature, the solar system, and the complexities of people themselves.

Like many cultures, Native Americans developed such myths and legends. Each Native American nation has its own distinctive body of tales that reflects its environment: the thunderous, unpredictable weather of the Pawnee in Nebraska; the searing sun of the Blackfeet in the Dakotas; and the high desert landscape of the Navajo. Some characters appear in the stories of all the Native American nations: the Great Spirit, the Sun, and the Morning Star. Human emotions such as jealousy, laziness, and pride are also a common subject in many of the legends.

In this collection, great care has been taken to attribute the origin of each story to the correct tribe and to authenticate the names of all the characters. In some cases, narratives have been simplified, but the essence of each tale has been maintained. In addition, all of the designs in the artwork have been researched so that they are true to the particular Native American nation from which that tale comes.

These stories have been handed down from father to son, mother to daughter, generation to generation. We hope that these remarkable tales enthrall and excite you as much as the first Native American listeners.

The Raven and the Moon

A Kwakiutl Tale

One day Raven learned of a strange box which belonged to an old fisherman and his daughter. The box was filled with a very bright light called the moon. Raven wanted that moon, and he vowed to get it. He changed himself into a leaf on the berry bush that grew near the fisherman's house. When the fisherman's daughter passed by, Raven fell into her body.

In time, the daughter gave birth to a baby with dark hair and a long hooked nose. As soon as he could crawl, the child knocked on the strange box and cried, "Moon, moon, shining moon."

Finally the fisherman said, "We may as well give him the ball of light to play with."

His daughter opened the strange box; inside it were many boxes, one nested in the other. When she opened the last box, the room was filled with light. The mother gave the ball of light to her son, who smiled happily.

The next night the child cried, "Stars, stars."

"He wants to see the night stars through the smoke hole, but it is covered by the roof board," said the girl to her father.

"Open the smoke hole," said her father.

No sooner had she opened it than the child changed back into the Raven he really was and flew off with the moon in his beak. He threw the moon up into the night sky, where it remains today.

The Dance of the Spirit Monster
A Kwakiutl Legend

Once, in a village beside a river, there lived a sad and ugly young man whose parents had died. In a nearby hut lived a hunter and his wife. One night the hunter's wife was awakened by a scratching sound on the roof. When she opened her eyes, she saw a large arm reaching out to grab the salmon they had caught that day.

"Wake up!" she whispered to her husband. "Someone is stealing our fish!"

The hunter reached for his bow and shot an arrow at the figure. There was a scream and the sound of something falling. The next morning the hunter saw that he had slain a spirit monster. This was an evil omen, and the hunter and his wife were afraid to tell anyone in the village.

Soon after this, the village heard mournful cries coming from down the river. The men paddled their canoes until they found an enormous spirit monster wailing on a rock.

"Why are you crying?" they asked.

"My son has disappeared," she wept.

The men were very frightened. "He may be dead," they said to themselves. "And she may think we killed him. We must leave this place before she tries to avenge his death." They paddled away as quickly as their arms could move their canoes.

But one sad and ugly young man remained.

Seeing that he was not frightened of her, the spirit monster trusted him. "Find my son and I will make you handsome and wealthy," she told him.

So the young man took the spirit monster to the hunter's hut. There they found the body of the spirit monster's son. Gently the spirit monster picked up her son and carried him to her richly decorated house. The young man followed in his canoe. The spirit monster softly placed her son on a bed and sprinkled some magic water over him. Instantly the arrow wound healed and he opened his eyes.

Then the spirit monster turned to the sad young man.

"Why are you sad?" she asked. He didn't answer, and so she gave him a carved mask. "With this mask you can become a spirit dancer and dance for your tribe," she told him. But still the young man was sad.

Next the spirit monster dropped some magic water on his face so that he became very handsome. But still the young man was sad.

Finally the young man spoke. "Spirit monster, you have regained your son," said the young man. "I am sad because my mother and father are dead."

"Take some of the water," said the spirit monster, "and throw it over your parents."

The young man left for the village, carefully cradling his pouch of magic water. That night his return was celebrated. The young man wore the carved mask and danced a spirit dance about the death of the son of the spirit monster. The hunter who had killed the spirit monster was jealous. "This is my dance!" he shouted.

The villagers were shocked.

"The spirit monster did not give this dance to the person who killed her son," the young man said, "but to the one who saved him."

Ashamed that their secret had been discovered, the hunter and his wife left the village forever.

The next day, in the light of the sun, the young man sprinkled the magic water over his mother and father, who opened their eyes and smiled. At last the young man was happy.

The Girl Who Married a Ghost

A Nisqualli Legend

A powerful chief of the Nisqualli had a beautiful daughter. Men came from near and far to ask for her hand in marriage, but the chief would not part with her. One unhappy suitor said as he was turned away, "The living are not good enough for the daughter of the chief. It would serve him right if the ghosts took her."

That night the chief saw many canoes coming toward him over the sea. A handsome young man jumped out of one of the canoes and said, "I have come to marry your daughter."

The chief hesitated, but the young man had brought so many presents that he could not refuse. His daughter was married that very night and left for her new home. Before long she arrived on an island with brightly painted houses and many people.

Her new husband said, "Tomorrow night I will show you the island, but now we must go to bed because the sun will soon rise."

Her husband fell asleep in an instant, but the girl waited for the sun. In the bright light, the houses looked old and faded. "How different everything seems at night," she thought. She turned to look at her husband.

The handsome young man was a skeleton on a rotted bed! Gasping in fright, the young bride ran out of her house to ask for help. But all the other houses were full of skeletons as well. "This must be the land of the dead," she said to herself. In her rush to leave the horrible place, she stumbled over some of the bones. When she reached the shore, the canoes crumbled at her touch. Frightened, the girl sat by the sea and cried.

At sunset the villagers came out of their houses. Some were injured where the girl had bumped into them. One man's head was crooked; another's foot pointed the wrong way.

"Look what you've done!" said her husband, handsome once more.

"I am sorry," said the girl, "but I did not know that you were one of the dead."

In the days that followed, the girl became used to waking by night and sleeping by day, and soon she gave birth to a son. "I would like my

parents to see him," she told her husband.

"If you must make the trip, do so. But do not undress our son in the daylight," he warned.

The girl was so happy to see her parents that she forgot to tell them of her husband's warning. In the morning, before the girl was awake, her mother went to play with her grandson. When she picked him up, she was shocked to see that his clothes were frayed and worn. "I have some new clothes for you," she said to the baby. But when she removed his clothes, there was only a skeleton in her arms. Her screams brought her daughter running. The girl gently picked up the bones and cradled them. "I must return to the land of the dead," she said. "That is where he belongs."

The chief and his wife wept as their daughter paddled away. And they never saw her again.

Michabo and the Flood

An Algonquin Creation Myth

This is the story of how Michabo accidentally destroyed the Earth and had to make the world all over again.

Michabo was a large and powerful spirit who lived before the world was as we know it today. One day he was hunting with his wolves. He sent them deep into the woods to search for food. After a long time the wolves did not return, so Michabo went to look for them.

Soon a raven flew by. "Have you seen my wolves?" Michabo asked the raven.

"They jumped into the lake," said the raven.

Michabo leaped into the lake to look for his wolves, but he forgot how big he was.

When he came to the surface, Michabo discovered that he had caused the lake to overflow and flood the entire world.

Eager to repair the damage, Michabo called to the raven again. "Please find me some earth," he said.

The raven searched the lake, but the water was too deep and he could not find any.

Out of the corner of his eye, Michabo saw an otter swim past. He called to the otter, "Please find me some earth."

The otter dived deep, but the water was too cloudy and he could not find any.

Out of the corner of his eye, Michabo saw a muskrat. "Please find me some earth," Michabo begged the muskrat. So the muskrat dived deep. He dived even deeper than the otter. He was under the water for so long that Michabo grew worried. But at last the muskrat emerged from the water and handed Michabo a tiny mound of earth.

Michabo rolled the earth around and around in his hands, and the tiny ball grew and grew and grew until it became the world we know today.

Morning Star's Son

A Blackfoot Legend

One day Morning Star looked down from the heavens and saw a beautiful girl named Soatsaki. He lifted her up to the sky to be his wife. Soatsaki soon gave birth to a son, Little Star.

In gratitude, Soatsaki's mother-in-law, the Moon, gave her a digging stick but warned, "Do not dig up the sacred turnip." But Soatsaki was curious and dug up the turnip, leaving a deep hole in the heavens. Before she could look through it, she was discovered by her father-in-law, the Sun. In a blaze of fury, he banished Soatsaki to Earth, along with Little Star. Soatsaki soon died of a broken heart.

Little Star was brought up by Soatsaki's tribe, the Blackfeet. But they made fun of him because the Sun's blaze of anger had left its mark on his cheek. When he was older, Little Star fell in love with the chief's daughter. She also laughed at his scar.

"My grandfather, the Sun, will remove it," he said.

"How can you be related to the Sun?" she asked, and laughed even more.

But Little Star was determined to prove his true identity, so he set off on a journey to find the Sun.

Finally Little Star reached the House of the Sun. There he found his father, Morning Star, in a deadly fight with seven gigantic birds. Little Star rushed to his side and killed all seven with his club.

The Sun was impressed with his grandson and rewarded him by removing the scar. He also gave Little Star some raven's feathers to prove his kinship with the Sun.

When Little Star returned to his tribe, the people saw the raven's feathers and Little Star's unscarred face and knew he was truly descended from the Sun. He married the chief's daughter, whom he loved, and, like his father, took his wife to live with him in the sky.

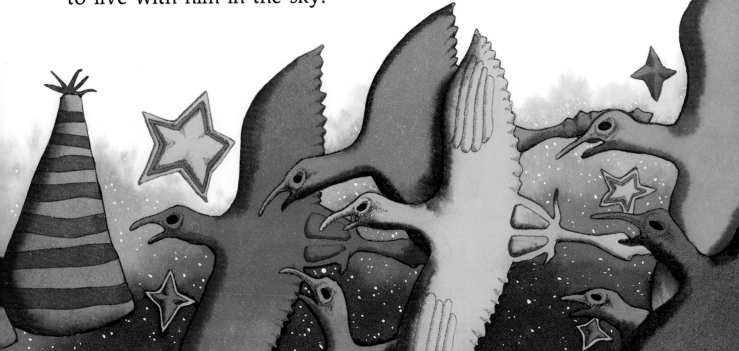

The Lazy Boy
A Kwakiutl Legend

Once there was a lazy boy who never hunted or fished with the others. The people in the tribe laughed at him and called him names as they went off to hunt. But, as soon as they left, the lazy boy washed with magical herbs that made him strong.

The people began to have trouble. The forest and mountains started to crush their homes, forcing the people to leave. As the last canoe was pushed from the shore, the lazy boy awoke and saw what was happening.

He stretched, then he uprooted trees and pushed them against the mountains, creating land once again. Returning to the awestruck people, the lazy boy yawned and went back to sleep. Not long after this, the evil spirits began to flatten the hills and mountains, stopping the rivers from flowing. The people woke the young man.

He called to a loon, "Tell my grandfather that I need great strength to push back the mountains."

When the loon returned, the boy knew his grandfather had sent him the magical power. He heaved back the mountains and broke them apart, allowing the rivers to flow. Then he fell asleep. The people rejoiced and revered him as the greatest and strongest of men.

One night a canoe landed and a stranger stepped ashore. "I have come for our great master," he said. He went to the lazy boy, who was, of course, asleep. "Your grandfather is ill and needs you. Your mission here is finished."

The young man said, "My grandfather holds up the Earth on a long pole, but now he is weak. I must take over for him. You will be safe."

Now, whenever the young man moves his feet or arms, he causes earthquakes and storms. And when men wish to send him a message, they ask the loon to carry it.

Tirawa Creates the People

A Pawnee Creation Myth

Soon after the Earth was created, the greatest god, Tirawa, spoke to the other gods. "I shall create people and a place for them to live and be happy, and you must protect them." Here is what he did:

Tirawa sent clouds, winds, thunder, and lightning to the gods. "They will prepare the Earth for the people," he said.

Then Tirawa asked the clouds to blanket the Earth. He dropped a pebble on the clouds to make a hole. The gods looked down through the hole and saw the Earth was covered with water.

Tirawa commanded the four gods holding up the sky to beat the waters. So the gods beat the waters until they parted, revealing the Earth below. The four gods were pleased and sang a jubilant song: "Mankind shall live there!" Their singing was so beautiful that the clouds, winds, thunder, and lightning crashed together in a huge thunderstorm. Lightning hit the Earth and carved valleys and mountains.

When the storm died down, the four gods sang again. This time a milder storm gathered and the Earth was covered with trees.

The gods began their third song, and a storm caused the rivers to overflow and water the Earth. The fourth and last song caused the grasses and plants to grow.

When the gods had finished their work, Tirawa was pleased. Then a son was born to Shakuru, god of the sun, and Pah, goddess of the moon, and a daughter was born to Big Star and Bright Star. They were the first people. Both children were carefully placed on the Earth, where, as Tirawa had commanded, they were cared for by the gods.

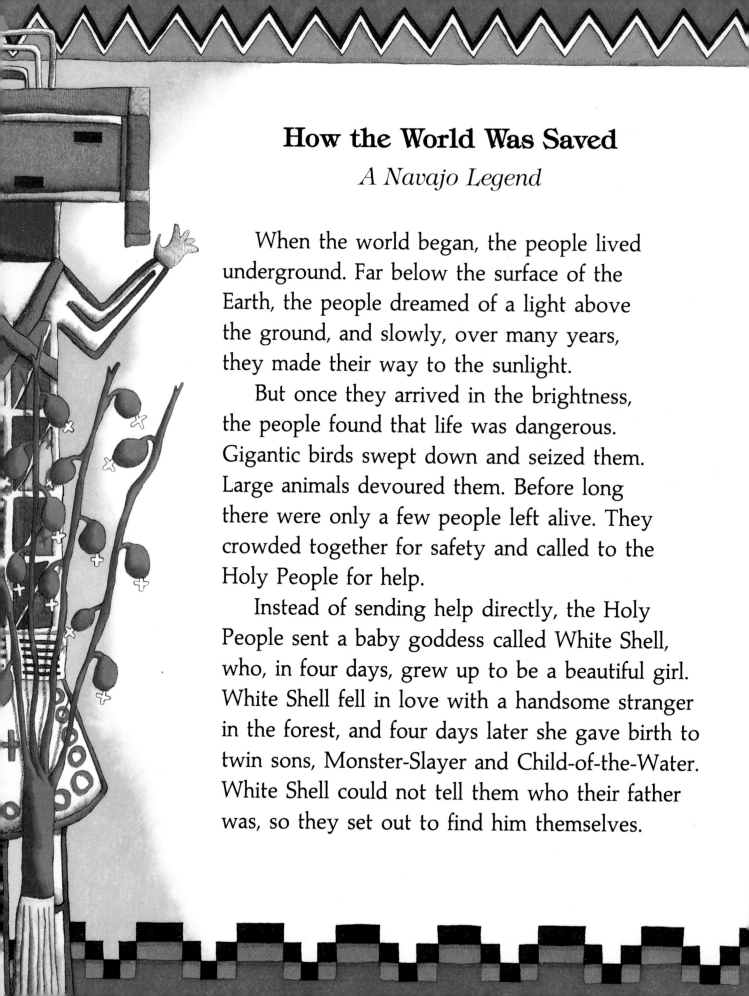

How the World Was Saved

A Navajo Legend

When the world began, the people lived underground. Far below the surface of the Earth, the people dreamed of a light above the ground, and slowly, over many years, they made their way to the sunlight.

But once they arrived in the brightness, the people found that life was dangerous. Gigantic birds swept down and seized them. Large animals devoured them. Before long there were only a few people left alive. They crowded together for safety and called to the Holy People for help.

Instead of sending help directly, the Holy People sent a baby goddess called White Shell, who, in four days, grew up to be a beautiful girl. White Shell fell in love with a handsome stranger in the forest, and four days later she gave birth to twin sons, Monster-Slayer and Child-of-the-Water. White Shell could not tell them who their father was, so they set out to find him themselves.

On their search they met Spider Woman, who told them that they were children of the Sun and gave them some feathers to help them on their journey. With these feathers they were able to leap over huge walls, free themselves from grasping reeds, and dodge crushing rocks.

Finally they reached the House of the Sun, which was set in the middle of a vast lake. This time the feathers couldn't help them cross—the distance was too great.

"Why do you want to go to the House of the Sun?" asked an old man standing at the edge of the lake.

"He is our father," replied the twins. So the old man created a rainbow bridge over the lake for the brothers to cross.

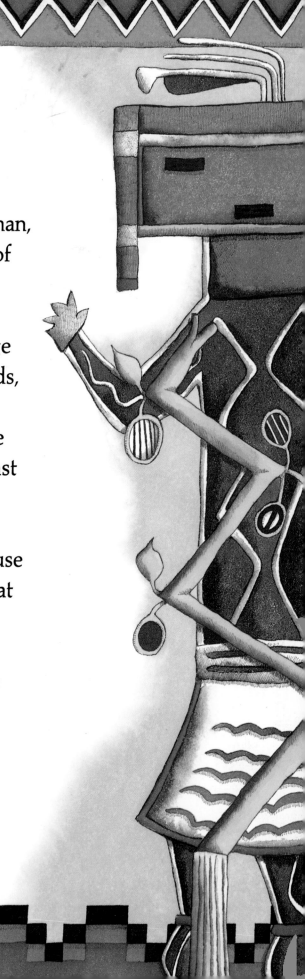

The House of the Sun was magnificent. Its walls glowed blue and green and the roof shone a brilliant white. Bravely Monster-Slayer and Child-of-the-Water walked in.

At first the Sun did not believe that the boys were his children. He tested them by throwing them down a mountainside, but they survived. Then he tried tempting them with rich gifts of gold, turquoise, and shell, but they refused. Then finally he greeted them as his brave sons.

When they told him of the hardships being suffered by their people on Earth, he gave them weapons to fight the monsters and helped them find their way home.

Monster-Slayer and Child-of-the-Water fought and killed many monsters. Some, like Hunger and Death, survived, but from that time on the world was a much safer place.

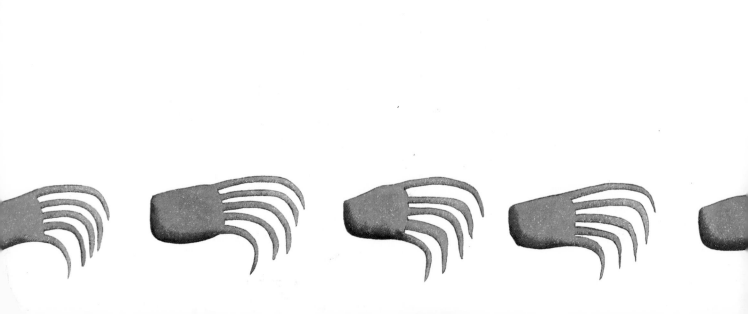